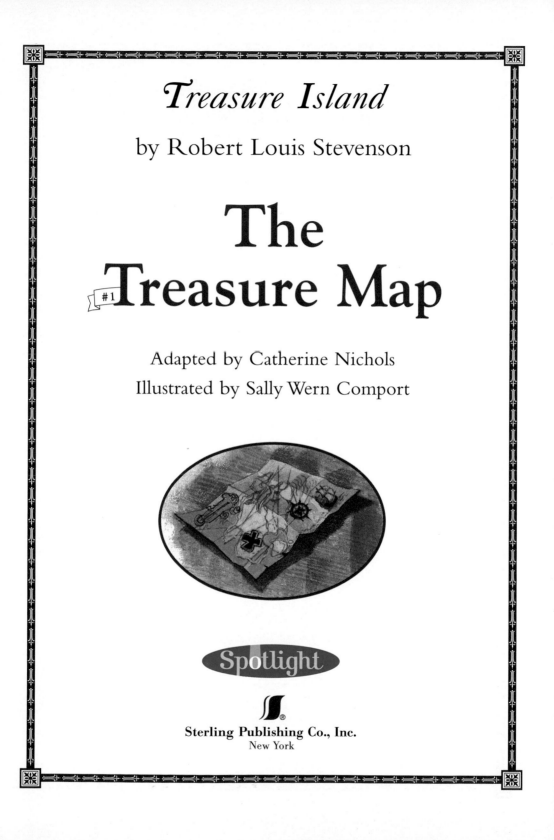

Treasure Island

by Robert Louis Stevenson

The
Treasure Map

#1

Adapted by Catherine Nichols

Illustrated by Sally Wern Comport

Spotlight

Sterling Publishing Co., Inc.
New York

visit us at www.abdopublishing.com

Reinforced library bound edition published in 2008 by Spotlight, a division of the ABDO
Publishing Group, 8000 West 78th Street, Edina, Minnesota 55439. Published by agreement
with Sterling Publishing Co., Inc.

Originally published and © 2006 by Barnes and Noble, Inc.
Illustrations © 2006 by Sally Wern Comport
Cover illustration by Sally Wern Comport

Library of Congress Cataloging-in-Publication Data
This title was previously cataloged with the following information:
Nichols, Catherine.
   Treasure Island. #1, The treasure map / by Robert Louis Stevenson ; adapted by
Catherine Nichols ; illustrated by Sally Wern Comport.
      p. cm. -- (Easy reader classics)
   Summary: A brief, simplified retelling of the episode in "Treasure Island" during which
Jim Hawkins gives Squire Tralawney a packet left behind by a sea captain staying at Jim's
parents' inn, and which pirates are trying to find.
   [1. Maps--Fiction. 2. Buried treasure--Fiction. 3. Pirates--Fiction. 4. Adventure and
adventurers--Fiction.] I. Comport, Sally Wern, ill. II. Stevenson, Robert Louis, 1850-1894.
III. Title.
PZ7.N5288 Tre 2006
[E]--dc22   2005027795
ISBN 978-1-59961-342-0 (reinforced library bound edition)

Contents

A Story to Tell

A young boy stood
in front of a door.
He put up his hand.
He wanted to knock,
but he was scared.
He put down his hand.
He was not sure
what he should do.

Squire Trelawney
was behind the door.
He was an important man.
Would he have time
to see a little boy
with a big story?

The boy thought about it.
He made up his mind.
The squire would want
to hear the story.

The boy knocked.

"Come in," a voice said.

The boy took a deep breath.

He opened the door.

The squire sat in a room
filled with many books.
Doctor Livesey
sat across from him.

"Who might you be?"
the squire asked the boy.
"Jim Hawkins," the boy said.
His voice was very tiny.

"Speak up, Jim,"
said the squire.
"Don't be scared,"
said the doctor.

The Sea Chest

Jim talked louder.
"Sirs," he said,
"I have a story to tell you."
"Tell us, my boy!"
said the squire.
"We are listening,"
the doctor said.
Jim took a deep breath.
His story came out
in one big rush.

"My family owns an inn.
Today pirates broke into it.
I was at the front desk.
I hid behind the desk.

"We had money on the desk,
but the pirates did not want it.
They wanted something else . . .

. . . something out of
the captain's sea chest!

"The captain was a sailor.

He had been staying at the inn.

He liked to sing songs

and tell stories about pirates.

"One day, he went away.

He left the chest behind.

"The pirates opened the chest.
They took everything out.
One pirate said they were
looking for a packet.
They could not find it.
They got angry.
They made a lot of noise.
Then they left."

"Where could the packet be?"
the squire asked.
Jim smiled and said,
"Here it is, sirs!"
He pulled it out
of his pocket.

X Marks the Spot

"*You* have it?"
asked the doctor.
"Yes," Jim said.
"Before the pirates came,
I saw it by the chest.
I wanted to give it
to the captain,
but he never came back.
I believe the squire
might be able to help."

"Let's see," said the doctor.
Jim gave him the packet.
The doctor cut it open.
Inside was a
sheet of paper.
It had a
drawing on it.
"It's a map!"
the squire said.

"The pirates wanted it,"
said the doctor.
"It must be important!"
"It is," the squire said.
"It's a treasure map!"

Jim pointed to
a large X on the map.
"What is this?" he asked.
"That, my boy,"
said the doctor,
"is where the treasure is!"

A Hunt for Treasure

The squire stood up.
He began to walk
around and around.
"This is exciting!" he said.
"Pirates' treasure.
I have always wanted
to find pirates' treasure!"

"We *could* go find it," the doctor said.
"I will buy a ship!" said the squire.

Jim watched the men
make their plans
to hunt for the treasure.
He wished he could go, too!

Jim didn't want to leave,
but he knew it was time
to go back to the inn.
He started to walk away.

"Where are you going?"
the squire asked Jim.

"Back to the inn," said Jim.

"Please wait," the squire said.

"We need a cabin boy
to work on the ship."

"Will you do it, Jim?"
asked the doctor.

"We will split the
treasure with you."
How Jim wanted to go—
but what about the inn?
They needed him there.

Jim could just see
all the gold and silver.
The money would be
a big help to his family...

. . . and Jim had always wanted
to go to sea.
He had always dreamed
of adventure.

"I will go home and see
if I can go," said Jim.
"I am sure it will be all right."
"My boy," the squire said,
"your adventures are beginning!"

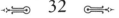